Mother-daughter duo,
Sally Gardner and Lydia Corry
are keen conservationists.
Sally is a Costa and Carnegie-
winning author and Lydia's debut
illustrated giftbook, *Eight
Princesses and a Magic Mirror*, was
a *Guardian* Best Book of 2019.

ID980602

The TINDIMS

of Rubbish Island

Sally Gardner & Lydia Corry

ZEPHYR

an imprint of Head of Zeus

First published in the UK by Zephyr,
an imprint of Head of Zeus, in 2020

Text copyright © Sally Gardner, 2020
Illustrations copyright © Lydia Corry, 2020

The moral right of Sally Gardner to be identified as the author of
this work and Lydia Corry to be identified as the illustrator of this
work has been asserted in accordance with the Copyright, Designs
and Patents Act of 1988.

All rights reserved. No part of this publication may be
reproduced, stored in a retrieval system, or transmitted in any form
or by any means, electronic, mechanical, photocopying, recording,
or otherwise, without the prior permission of both the copyright
owner and the above publisher of this book.

This is a work of fiction. All characters, organizations, and events
portrayed in this novel are either products of the author's
imagination or are used fictitiously.

9 7 5 3 4 6 8

A catalogue record for this book is available
from the British Library.

ISBN (PB): 9781838935672
ISBN (E): 9781838935689

Typesetting & design by Jessie Price

Printed and bound in Great Britain
by CPI Group (UK) Ltd, Croydon CR0 4YY

Head of Zeus Ltd
First Floor East
5–8 Hardwick Street
London EC1R 4RG

www.headofzeus.com

To our dearest
Fried Egg (also
known by the Long
Legs as Freya), the
greatest guide and
our trusted adviser
in all things Tindims.

From SG and LC

hello!

Chapter One

Where we meet
Skittle, one of the
young Tindims of
Rubbish Island, and
her furry, purry
pet, Pinch.

*S*kittle climbed out of bed, pulled back the curtains and couldn't believe what she saw. She had wished for snow for ages, and here it was. Big, thick snowflakes - lots of them. Rubbish Island, she thought, must have sailed into icy waters by mistake. She hadn't seen snow for so long she was worried it might have gone away.

'Wake up, Pinch,' she said.

Pinch was curled in an old jewellery box, his long, furry tail wrapped round him.

'It's Tunaday,' said Skittle, which is what Tindims call Tuesday. 'And look - it's snowing. Really huge flakes. That means Rubbish Island will turn white.

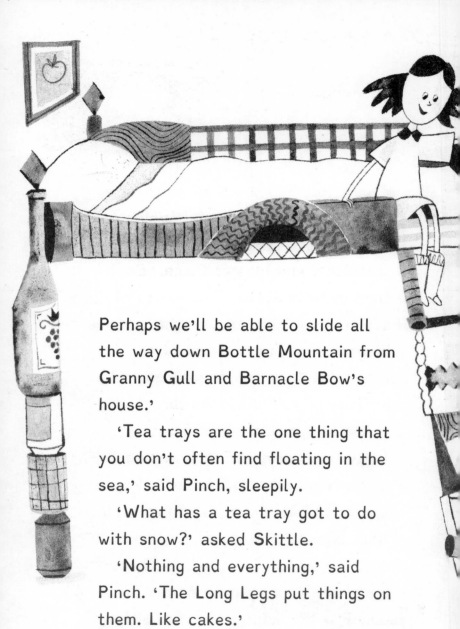

Perhaps we'll be able to slide all
the way down Bottle Mountain from
Granny Gull and Barnacle Bow's
house.'

'Tea trays are the one thing that
you don't often find floating in the
sea,' said Pinch, sleepily.

'What has a tea tray got to do
with snow?' asked Skittle.

'Nothing and everything,' said
Pinch. 'The Long Legs put things on
them. Like cakes.'

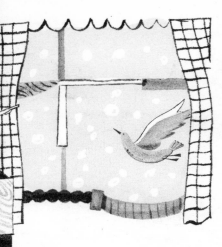

'Why?'
asked Skittle.

'I don't know,' said Pinch. 'But
they do.'

And they burst out laughing. They
laughed down to the tips of their
toes until their tummies jelly-jiggled.

'They're flat,' said Pinch.

'What are flat?' said Skittle.

'Tea trays,' said Pinch, wiping
his eyes with his tail. 'That's why
they're grand for sliding down snowy
mountains.'

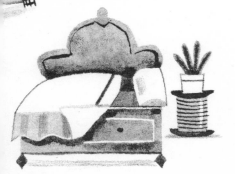

Skittle put on her red-and-white checked dress. She did up her useful belt, in which she kept a helpful hook and her best pencil.

Tindims are much smaller than humans, who they call the Long Legs. Human children they call the Little Long Legs.

She helped Pinch do up the buttons on his waistcoat. Paws and buttons don't mix.

Last of all, Skittle collected her toothbrush. The Long Legs use toothbrushes to brush their teeth, but Tindims have many more uses for them, such as polishing and scrubbing and other things that end in **ING**. She decided to leave it at home as this was a snowy sort of day, not an **ING** sort of day.

When they were quite ready, Skittle said, 'Do you know it's only two days until the Brightsea Festival?'

And with that happy thought they set off up the staircase to the kitchen.

As they went, they sang a Tindim song.

'Oh, the sun is shining on the sea.

What rubbish will the tide bring me?'

Skittle's house was
at the top of Rubbish
Island. If she stood
outside, she could see
the whole island. On one
side, the Lake of Still
Water and the Roo-
Roo Tree Wood. And
the craggy edges of the
island, right round to
Turtle Bay. On the other
side, all she could see
was Bottle Mountain.

Roo-Roo
trees

We find most things funny,
We laugh when times are good,
We laugh when times are bad,

The house itself was higgledy-piggledy.
Skittle's bedroom was downstairs and the
kitchen was upstairs. Pinch was counting
his steps and stopped on the seventh
stair. This was handy as he couldn't
count past ten. He had left something
important behind. He unrolled his tail all
the way back to the bedroom and picked
up his scarf. With one twitch he wrapped
it three times around his neck.

They sang as they went up the stairs.

We laugh when it is sunny,
We laugh when times are sad.'

Skittle stopped at the kitchen door.

She thought for a moment. 'Perhaps we should have sung *we don't laugh when times are bad or sad*?'

'That doesn't sound so good,' said Pinch. 'But I agree, it's all right to feel sad.'

'Yes,' said Skittle. 'But we're not sad today, not with the snow. Today is a day for laughter.'

'*That's a fact,*' said Pinch.

Chapter Two

In which we meet Skittle's mum, Admiral Bonnet, and her dad, Captain Spoons. And we learn that Tindims are top recyclers.

*N*ot long ago, Captain Spoons, Skittle's dad, had fished a large plastic bag out of the sea. Inside were five soggy boxes with the word **CRACKERS** on the lid. Admiral Bonnet, Skittle's mum, had no idea what **CRACKERS** meant, but she liked the colourful paper hats inside. As with all wet things, they had to be dried. Only then would the Tindims know if they were useful. Some things just stay a mess, but luckily not the paper hats.

'It shows us,' said Admiral Bonnet, 'that the Long Legs are a strange bunch.'

Skittle's mum
and dad had used
the paper hats
to wallpaper the
kitchen and it
looked most jolly.
Captain Spoons had
made a light from
the plastic trinkets
they'd found in the
crackers and hung it
above the kitchen table.
Their table was made from
driftwood and their chairs
from plastic cups.

'Good neeptide, you two,'
said Captain Spoons. That's
the Tindim way of saying good
morning.

Captain Spoons was in
charge of the frying pan. He
tossed a pancake into the
air. Skittle grabbed a plate
and caught the pancake just
in time.

The Tindims were recyclers. In fact,
they were recyclers well before the word
had even found a plastic bag to crawl
out of. They'd been around as long as the
Vikings. That's a very long time indeed.
The Vikings, being hairy and furious,
had sea battles. It was from a piece of
a longboat shipwreck that the Tindims
began to build Rubbish Island. Then came
sailors and pirates, and galleons with tall
sails and treasure chests. They'd left lots
floating about for the Tindims to keep
building with.

The Long Legs didn't know about the
Tindims. Years passed and times changed.

Instead of glass and wood,
along came plastic in different shapes
and sizes. The Tindims began to realise
that everything they thought was useful
was rubbish to the Long Legs. For a long
time, that didn't matter. They carried on
recycling. Their motto was 'Rubbish today
is treasure tomorrow'. But now with the
sea full of plastic bottles the Tindims
wondered if they could still
be called treasure.

The Tindims made a pile
of plastic bottles. The
pile became a mound, the
mound became a hill, the
hill became a mountain!

Their island had always
floated, bobbing in the
waves, and it was the job
of Admiral Bonnet and
Captain Spoons to steer
it safely through the
oceans.

Captain Spoons'
wheelhouse was at the
top of a tower that he'd
built onto their house. He
reached it by way of the
kitchen and a twisty-
turny staircase. From
there, he made sure

the island didn't bump into rocks, cruise
liners or Long Leg divers. A thin tube
near the captain's chair went all the way
down through the island to the engine
room. Captain Spoons was able to talk
to Spokes in the engine room. But right
now, there was no point in pulling up the
anchor and starting the engine because of
Bottle Mountain.

Captain Spoons said, 'We shouldn't be in a snowstorm.'

'We should leave tomorrow if we're to find some sunshine for the Brightsea Festival,' said Admiral Bonnet.

'Yes,' said Skittle. 'The sacks will be handed out then.'

That is the part the Tindims most looked forward to. On the neeptide

of Brightsea Eve each Tindim is given a
sack full of things that had been fished
out of the sea. It is up to each Tindim
to use what they find in the sack to
make fish costumes. The Tindim with the
emptiest sack is crowned the winner.

'But the problem is Bottle Mountain
– it's blocking our view of the sea,' said
Captain Spoons. 'It's impossible to see
where we're going.'

It was a problem that cast a long shadow over the little Tindims. No matter how hard they tried to laugh it off, it wouldn't go away. And as Admiral Bonnet said, 'If you can't laugh at something that worries you, the worry only gets bigger.'

'*That's a fact actually,*' said Pinch.

Chapter Three

Where we discover
there are too
many plastic
bottles, even for
the Tindims.

Once upon a time, the Long Legs put messages into glass bottles and threw them out to sea. It had been a hobby of Hitch Stitch's to catch the glass bottles as they floated by. She would read the messages and then find the right tide and hope they would be washed up on the right shore. It was a puzzle how they would find the right person. But Hitch Stitch said the Long Legs must have known that when

they put messages in bottles, otherwise
what would be the point? A question to
which no Tindim could think of an answer.

Now it was plastic bottles
that were worrying Captain
Spoons and Admiral Bonnet.
There were lots and lots
of them, with no
messages inside,
just writing on the
outside. Words like
STILL, SPARKLING
and most baffling
of all, WATER.

The Tindims had no idea what these words meant. And as no Tindim in their long history had ever met a Long Leg, there was no one to ask. It was another mystery among the many mysteries about the Long Legs.

Granny Gull thought that WATER was what the Long Legs put *in* the plastic bottles. Captain Spoons thought that was daft. Admiral Bonnet thought it was plain silly. But whatever the Tindims thought, there were more plastic bottles than they knew what to do with.

26

First, they'd made furniture with them,
then they'd built underwater rooms. Still
the plastic bottles washed up on shore.
Every day there were more.

Granny Gull and Barnacle Bow decided
to live on Bottle Mountain. Barnacle
Bow had his heart set on living in a boat.
Granny Gull had her heart set on living
in a house. As neither wanted the other
to be broken-hearted, they'd built a
houseboat.

Whether it was hot or rainy, they'd hook the things needed out of the waves. Granny Gull and Barnacle Bow sorted plastic bricks into different sizes and colours. Once they were sure they had enough, they built their houseboat and they lived happily at the top of Bottle Mountain.

Chapter Four

Where we meet
Brew and his family.
Where Brew gets
stuck and Skittle
comes to the rescue.

Apart from Pinch, Brew was Skittle's best friend on Rubbish Island. Brew was younger than she was and believed in magic. When he grew up he was going to be a magician and make the plastic bottles disappear. Except for Bottle Mountain, as Granny Gull and Barnacle Bow lived there.

Brew's family lived not far from the Roo-Roo Tree Woods, forty-seven steps from Skittle and Pinch's home. Their bungalow was called 'All-Sorts' because it had been built from all sorts of things fished from the sea.

It had a garden with two Roo-Roo trees. Roo-Roo trees have shiny, flat leaves that are good for making hats. Their green fruits are hairy on the

outside, but once they've been peeled
they taste of mangoes and strawberries.
They make a delicious drink, loved by all
Tindims.

That Tunaday, Brew had been excited
to see the island turn white. He'd run
outside wearing just his fishing-net cape.

It wasn't enough to keep him warm and he quickly went back indoors.

His mum, Mug, whose name came from the hat she wore, had made Brew a bubble-wrap coat. He looked just like a roll of bubble wrap.

'I'm on bottle duty with Skittle today,' said Brew. 'But the trouble is, I can't move in this.'

Mug agreed that it wasn't the best coat she'd ever made. But she'd had hardly any time.

'No one warned us we were heading into a snowstorm,' she said. 'We aren't prepared for cold weather. What is Captain Spoons doing?'

'It's because Bottle Mountain is in the way,' said Brew's dad, Jug. His name also came from his hat. 'It's just too high.'

The other Tindims thought Jug was a fountain of facts. He collected them from magazines and manuals he found on the beach. So Mug thought it might be worth asking, 'How can we make these plastic bottles disappear?'

But even Jug didn't have an answer to that.

'Search my tea-strainer,' he replied. 'The Long Legs are a strange bunch.'

'The Brightsea Festival never takes place in cold waters and we're stuck here,' said Mug. 'Something has to happen. I'm filling the sacks tomorrow.'

Jug checked the calendar hanging on the wall.

'Yesterday was Monkday. Today is Tunaday,' he said. 'And tomorrow is Winkleday when you hand out the sacks.'

'Oh dear,' said Mug, handing Brew
the wooden spoon that he took with him
everywhere. 'That's soon.'

Brew was too excited about the snow
to think of anything else. 'See you later,'
he said and opened the front door. But
when he tried to go out, he got jammed
in the doorway.

Mug and Jug did their best. They
pushed and pulled with all their might,
but no matter how hard they tried Brew
was wedged tight. Baby Cup thought it

was the funniest thing she'd ever seen.

'That's how Skittle found him.

'What are you doing?' she asked.

'I'm stuck,' said Brew.

Skittle took out her useful hook. 'I hate to pop your bubbles,' she said. She went to work, pop-pop-popping.

'More, more,' said Baby Cup, who liked the sound of all the popping.

Brew began to laugh. 'It tickles,' he said, and he laughed so much that he shot out of his coat and out of the doorway.

'You can't wear that,' said Skittle, helping Brew to his feet.

Skittle was sensibly dressed in a sailcloth coat. Pinch was wearing a knitted string jumper. Both looked as cosy as hot water bottles.

'Here,' said Skittle. She undid her backpack and held out a coat made of knitted plastic bags. It had bottle top buttons down the front. 'Mum thought you might like this.'

'It's just the ticket,' said Brew.

Chapter Five

In which we meet
Spokes in the Engine
Room. Skittle asks
him if he has a
tea tray and Brew
makes him laugh.

rew loved buttons as much as he loved magic. He collected buttons – or rather, he collected anything that could be made into buttons, such as bottle tops and shells. His dad had given him a tin filled with buttons that the Long Legs had thrown away. It was Brew's treasure. He'd told Skittle, and no one else, that he believed they had magical powers. A bit like his collection of wooden spoons. Brew thought they were wands in disguise.

All wrapped up and as warm as buttered toast, they set off down the steps to the Engine Room.

Skittle, Pinch
and Brew agreed
they'd ask Spokes if
he could help them find
a tea tray. He lived at the
bottom of the island near the
sea edge. Spokes was in charge of
the Engine Room and making sure
the island didn't run out of power.
Although it bobbed about in the sea,
it did at least bob with purpose.

When it came to mechanical and
practical things there was nothing Spokes
couldn't do, if you asked him nicely.
He never said, 'No,' or 'Not now,' or 'I
haven't got time.' He would listen with
his big ears, then take off his cap.

He'd scratch his head and say, 'Glad
you asked me that – it's on my list
of things to do.' All he asked
was that you made him laugh.

On their way, Brew tried
to remember Jug's joke so
that he could tell Spokes.

'Why does a mountain never get cold?'
he asked Skittle.

'I don't know,' said Skittle.

'Bother. Neither do I,' said Brew. 'I've
forgotten the answer.'

Pinch piped up. 'Because it has a hat
on its head – and *that's a fact.*'

They all laughed.

'That may not be the right answer,'
said Pinch. 'It's just the way I tell them.'

When they reached the bottom of the
steps, they heard whistling. There was
only one Tindim who could whistle and
that was Spokes.

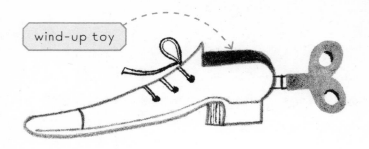

wind-up toy

Spokes' Engine Room was full of things. Some were hanging up, some were kept in boxes labelled **MIGHT COME IN HANDY** and **NEARLY USEFUL**.

The machine that powered the island was made of rubbish, of course. Here was the other end of the long pipe that ran up to Captain Spoons' wheelhouse so that Spokes could speak to him. This was very important when it came to steering the

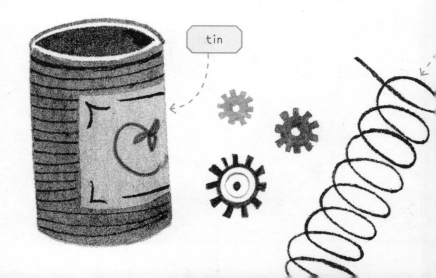

tin

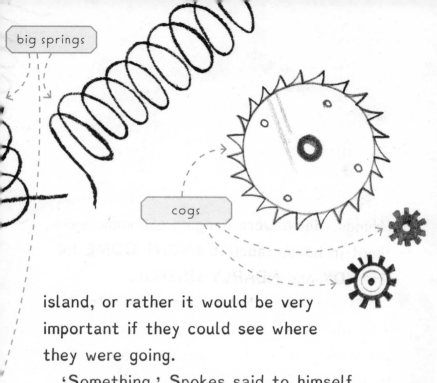

big springs

cogs

island, or rather it would be very important if they could see where they were going.

'Something,' Spokes said to himself, 'will have to be done.'

That morning he was trying to work out how Captain Spoons might see over or around or through Bottle Mountain.

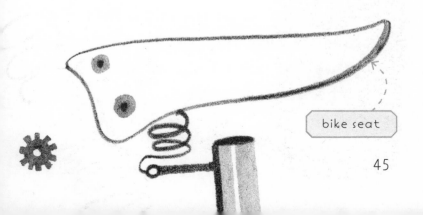

bike seat

45

Spokes looked up the second he heard
the young Tindims on the steps. He had
excellent hearing. He could hear a turtle
cough when it was far out at sea.

'Can I help?' he asked.

'We were wondering if you had a tea tray?' said Skittle.

'Or two,' added Pinch.

'Glad you asked me that,' said Spokes.

'For sliding down the mountain,' said Brew. And he told Spokes how he'd got stuck in the doorway.

'A tea tray,' said Spokes, laughing. 'Leave it with me. It's on my list.'

Chapter Six

In which Hitch Stitch
hooks a splendid red,
flattish thing.

itch Stitch, the queen of knots, lived at Turtle Bay.
At night, she would lie in her hammock and wonder who hung the lights in the sky. Perhaps they had a hook like hers to catch them with. Often, as she was falling asleep, she thought she wouldn't mind the job of star catcher.

On the next floor down was Hitch Stitch's sitting room. A stove kept it snug and warm. Another floor down was her kitchen.

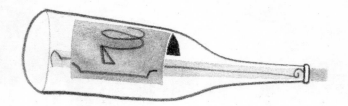

But today, when Hitch Stitch woke up,
she couldn't see out of her glass roof.
She went to the window.

'Snow!' she said and
started to laugh.
It shouldn't be
snowing, but
it did make the
island look magical.

Hitch Stitch's job was to hook bottles
from the sea. Nowadays, all she seemed
to pull from the waves were plastic
bottles. Too many had fish trapped inside.

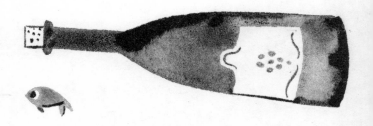

They swam into the bottles when they were small and before you could say 'shrivel a shark' the tide had carried them far from home. Not knowing where they were, they stayed in the bottles and grew too big to escape.

The fish were taken to Ethel B Dina at the Fish Hospital. The bottles were taken up Bottle Mountain to Barnacle Bow later.

'Plastic bottles long legs, please,'

When Skittle, Pinch and Brew arrived on the jetty, Hitch Stitch was already there. She'd hooked two plastic bottles with fish in them and three without.

'Be careful,' said Hitch Stitch. 'It's icy. We don't want anyone falling in. That wouldn't be funny.' She handed Brew a net. 'I'll hook, you catch.'

Brew caught another bottle and so the neeptide passed happily, while the snow

'They're not meant
To float in seas.'

fell and **Skittle** sang one of **Ethel B
Dina**'s ditties to keep them warm.

'I've been thinking,' said **Skittle**,
using her helpful hook to fish their
twenty-first bottle out of the
water. 'We should contact the **Long
Legs** and ask them to stop throwing
plastic bottles into the sea. I know
we haven't done it before, but don't
you think that now's the time?'

55

'No, no,' said Hitch Stitch. 'Not a good idea. The Long Legs are big and cross, and they don't laugh.'

'But think,' said Skittle, 'we could ask the Long Legs all these questions. Maybe they don't know they're throwing away treasure? If they did, they might stop.'

That's a fact, said Pinch.

They were about to stop for hightide, which means lunch to you and me, when they saw a splendid red, flattish thing.

'What is it?' asked Brew, once they'd dragged it ashore.

'It's a red, flattish thing,' said

Hitch Stitch. 'It's splendid!'

'Come on,' said Skittle, lunch forgotten, 'let's play Turn to Treasure.'

It's a game Tindims love to play. They imagine all the different ways what they fish out of the sea might be turned into something useful that becomes treasure.

'A flag,' said Pinch.

'A sack,' said Skittle.

'A red tent,' said Hitch Stitch.

'Wait a minute,' said Brew. 'Isn't it an enormous balloon?'

'Yes, it is,' said the others.

'If it's an enormous balloon,' said Brew, 'we might be able to fill it with hot air. Then it could take one of us up and over the top of the mountain.'

'That's a winning idea,' said Skittle.

It was then that something inside the enormous balloon began to wriggle.

Chapter Seven

We meet Ethel B Dina, an opera singer, who sings to the fish to make them feel better.

Rubbish Island was almost as deep as it was tall. Under the island the Tindims had built different kinds of rooms. The main rubbish sorting room was there, and the library.

Next door was Ethel B Dina's pretty flat, where she could see fish swimming past her underwater windows.

That neeptide she dressed and put on her lifesaver belt. Her favourite was in the shape of a blow-up swan. It was a little tight round the middle and she only wore it on special occasions.

When she was ready she went to work
in the fish hospital and noticed it was
rather chilly. The hospital had different
wards for different fish and sea creatures.
Only when they were strong enough did
the fish swim home - on the right tide,
of course. The octopus ward was empty
apart from three baby octopuses. There
were coral beds for the fish and below
was the Garden of Wonders, as Ethel B
Dina called it. She wore her lifesaver to
float among the turtles and sing a turtle-
ish lullaby to them.

'Rock-a-bye, turtle your sea is green,
Father's a nobleman, mother's a queen,
Ethel B Dina wears lifesaver rings
And in her sea garden, that's
where she sings.'

It had just turned floodtide, that's afternoon to you and me, when Skittle knocked on the hospital door.

'My still and sparkling darlings, what have you there?' said Ethel B Dina.

Hitch Stitch was carefully carrying the red balloon with the something wriggly inside it.

'A balloon,' said Pinch.

Ethel B Dina took her time emptying the water from the balloon into a tank and out popped a rainbow starfish.

'Isn't it beautiful!' said Skittle.

'It's rare to find a rainbow starfish,' said Brew.

'*That's a fact,*' said Pinch.

'I think,' said Ethel B Dina, 'that we should let the still and sparkling darling recover. Meanwhile, we'll rescue the fish from the plastic bottles.'

Everyone stood back. Pinch wrapped his tail around his head eight times as Ethel B Dina began to sing.

Before you could say
'frolicking fishes,' the plastic
bottles had split perfectly in two and the
fish were free to swim about in the
sink. Quite how Ethel B Dina did
it was a mystery – but it worked.

Once she had tucked up the
fish in their tanks, they went back
to see the rainbow starfish. It had
perked up and was looking at them
with shining eyes.

'Do you speak
starfish?' Skittle
asked Ethel B Dina.
'Of course,' she said.

'Now, my still and sparkling darlings, why don't you go and play in the snow?'

'We need a tea tray, so we can slide down the mountain,' said Pinch.

'We asked Spokes,' said Skittle, 'but I don't think he has one.'

'He does,' said Ethel B Dina.

'How do you know?' asked Brew.

'Because I gave him one to give to you. Now go and enjoy yourselves.'

They left Ethel B Dina and Hitch Stitch singing a sort of starfish lullaby.

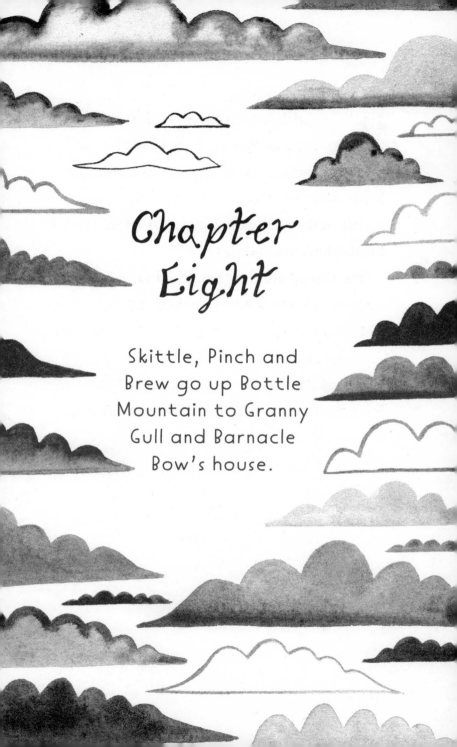

Chapter Eight

Skittle, Pinch and Brew go up Bottle Mountain to Granny Gull and Barnacle Bow's house.

*I*t would have taken Skittle, Pinch and Brew the rest of the day to climb Bottle Mountain if Bottle Mountain hadn't had a cable car. Without it, Granny Gull and Barnacle Bow wouldn't have been able to live there either. Granny Gull could still hop, skip and turn somersaults, but climbing Bottle Mountain was too much for a Tindim of any age.

To get round this, Spokes and Barnacle Bow had put up sailing boat masts strung with ropes that ran from Captain Spoon's house to Granny Gull's at the top of Bottle Mountain.

The cable car was made from parts of packing cases and was worked by pulleys. Hitch Stitch had tied all the knots.

Skittle, Pinch and Brew couldn't wait to try out the tea tray. Admiral Bonnet pulled the bell for the cable car and it came whizzing down from Bottle Mountain. With a jerk and a wobble, off they went. Below them was the sea. Up in the sky, Granny Gull and Barnacle Bow's colourful houseboat floated in snow clouds.

That afternoon was the best ever.
They all laughed so much as they whizzed
down the mountain on the tea tray. Even
Granny Gull had a go.

By the time they'd gone down the
mountain five times and up again in the
cable car, they were tired and hungry.

'Tea,' said Granny Gull.

Inside the houseboat it was warm and cosy. The fire crackled and the walls were lined with Granny Gull's paintings of tins.

The round table was laid for tea. Tindims like to do tea properly. They always sit down to enjoy it together. There were muffins, toast, three kinds of bread – one with seeds – four different jams, and Fruit Surprise cakes.

Barnacle Bow said that although the snow was fun and lovely to look at, the island really shouldn't have bobbed so far north into such cold seas.

'What we need,' he
said, 'is something
to lift one of us
into the sky so
that whoever is
at the end of that
something could
call down and tell
us where we should be
going.'

'We've got it!' cried Brew, Pinch and
Skittle together.

'You have?' said Granny Gull.

'Yes, it's a red balloon,' said Brew.
'With a rainbow starfish inside.'

'A balloon?' said Barnacle Bow. 'That's proper treasure.' He stood up. 'I am going to look at this balloon right away. And, by the way, I've never seen a rainbow starfish.'

'Off you go then,' said Granny Gull. She brought out a box of decorations. 'You three can help me. These have to go up in time for the Brightsea Festival.'

Skittle, Pinch and Brew spent the rest of the floodtide unwrapping last year's decorations.

'There's nothing better than remembering what you've forgotten,' said Brew. 'Like these starfish decorations I made.'

★

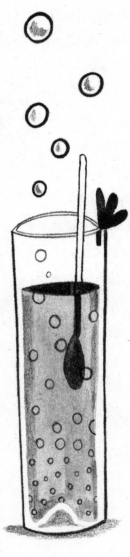

The festival is held once a year when the Tindims thank the sea for the gifts it gives them. That's rubbish to you and me, but not to the Tindims. Their motto, as you know, is 'Rubbish today is treasure tomorrow'. Well, that used to be their motto, but these days rubbish was becoming more of a challenge.

The festival lasts two days. Broom the gardener makes his famous Roo-Roo Pop, a hot drink which is probably the fizziest and bubbliest in the world.

On the ebbtide
of Brightsea Eve, the
Tindims put up decorations,
open their sacks and start to
make costumes in the shape of
different fish.

On Brightsea Day itself, they finish
their costumes and gather on the beach
dressed for the feast. Every Tindim worth
his or her fishing net looks forward to
the festival more than anything. Now it
was only a day until Brightsea Day. The
Tindims didn't feel it would be quite right
to have the festival in the snow. They
had to find a way for Captain Spoons to
steer them to some sunshine.

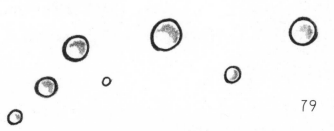

The light had begun to fade. Skittle and Brew put on their boots, hats, coats and mittens. Skittle buttoned Pinch into his warm waistcoat. Then they said goodnight to Granny Gull, rang the bell for the cable car and went home to bed.

Chapter Nine

We meet Broom the gardener, who is finding it tricky to keep his plants warm.

*I*t snowed so much that night that next day, Winkleday, Wednesday to the Long Legs, Captain Spoons couldn't open his front door.

'This is a fine thing to happen on Brightsea Eve,' he said.

He was about to climb out of the window when there was a knock on the door that he couldn't open.

'Is that you, Brew? We're snowed in,' said Skittle.

'No,' came the voice of Broom, the island's gardener. 'I've cleared the path. The door should open now.'

Captain Spoons ran to the front
door just as Broom pushed it open. The
Captain flew headfirst into the snow.
They all laughed so much that Broom
forgot why he'd come to see them.

Broom was long, in a tallish, furry
kind of way. He was slightly shy and a
beautiful shade of green. He had the best
laugh of any of the Tindims, deep, round
and so funny it often gave him hiccups.

'Plants,' he would say, 'are friends
with much to give.' And it was because

of Broom and his plants that the Tindims were very well fed.

He remembered he'd come to ask how long it would be before the island moved away from the cold weather.

Broom lived in a tall greenhouse, about twelve long steps or fifteen bottles from the orchard and his allotment. Or, he used to, but now it was full of containers of all shapes and sizes, each home to a small plant he'd brought inside out of the snow. And now Broom was homeless.

'I do believe that Pinch, Skittle and Brew found proper treasure yesterday which may be able to help us,' said Captain Spoons.

'It's a balloon,' said
Admiral Bonnet. 'It's
rather grand and red.
We must find a way
to fill it with hot air
so that it floats up high.
Hitch Stitch will tie Jug to
the balloon. He will be able
to see over the top of Bottle
Mountain and tell Captain
Spoons which direction to
steer in. Any ideas, Broom?'

Broom took off his hat.
'Hmmm,' he said. 'We should
ask Jug. He knows everything.
But let me think.'

The room fell quiet. At last,
he said, 'Maybe the fish could
help. What if Spokes made a
funnel that we put under the

sea with a long tube attached to the balloon?'

'Then what?' said Captain Spoons.

'Then,' said Broom, 'Ethel B Dina asks all the fish to blow bubbles into the funnel so the balloon fills with warm air.'

'That's it,' said Admiral Bonnet.

'That's it,' said Captain Spoons.

'Is it?' said Broom. 'Perhaps we should speak to Jug...'

'All hands, all hands on deck!' called Admiral Bonnet. 'Skittle, fetch Brew and go and tell Ethel B Dina she must sing to the fish and ask for their help. Oh – and take these.' She handed Skittle three sacks. 'Give them to Mug so she can fill them with treasure for the fish costumes.'

Chapter Ten

Ethel B Dina sings a
very special song and
the fish listen.

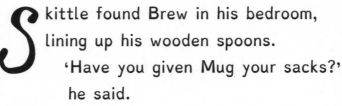

S kittle found Brew in his bedroom,
lining up his wooden spoons.

'Have you given Mug your sacks?'
he said.

'Yes,' said Skittle. 'But
what are you doing?'

'I was trying to see if
any of my wooden spoons
have magic in them.'

'Do they?' asked
Skittle.

'Search my teabag. I
don't think so.'

'Never mind,'
she said.

'Let's go,' said Pinch. 'We must tell
Ethel B Dina to sing to the fish.'

Brew picked up his favourite spoon
and they set off. It was cold again and
it somehow seemed that there was too
much snow, even to Brew and Skittle and
Pinch.

'It's not really the weather for the
Brightsea Festival,' said Skittle.

'N-n-n-o,' said Brew, his teeth
chattering.

Pinch had nearly disappeared, the snow was so deep. By the time they reached the Fish Hospital, he looked like a snow beast.

'There you are, my still and sparkling darlings,' said Ethel B Dina.

Ethel B Dina floated more than she walked. She wafted and she whirled. Between the wafting and the whirling, things got done.

'Broom has thought of a way to fill the balloon,' said Skittle.

'He has?' said Ethel B Dina. 'How?'

Skittle told her the plan.

Ethel B Dina thought for a moment. 'It would take a lot of fish bubbles to fill the balloon, but I might have the answer. There's a special friend of mine who could help.'

Ethel went to the Turtle Garden and sang a heartfelt song.

'I've put the message out there,' she said when she returned. 'Now all we can do is wait.'

She brought out freshly baked biscuits and a pot of glee, which is tea for a Tindim.

'Wait for what?' asked Skittle and Pinch.

Brew was staring at the rainbow starfish who now had its own tank.

'Look,' said Skittle.

A huge funnel was floating past the window.

'My idea will only work if the three octopuses are up to the job,' said Ethel B Dina.

'Up to what job?' asked Brew.

Before Ethel B Dina could reply, Spokes came in to ask if she'd sent a message to the fish.

'No,' said Ethel B Dina in a mysterious way. 'I sang to a mammal. And the octopuses are on standby, ready to help. As I said, all we can do is wait.'

'Wait for what?' asked Skittle, Pinch and Brew again. 'You still haven't said.'

'Better that it's a surprise,' said Ethel B Dina.

'I like surprises,' said Pinch.

'Could you give us a clue?' asked Brew.

'No,' said Ethel B Dina.

'Let's guess,' said Spokes. 'A mammal, you say, not a fish?'

Just then Pinch let out a loud cry. All the hairs on his body stood up straight.

'What's that?' he cried.

'That's what I've been waiting for,' said Ethel B Dina.

97

Chapter Eleven

In which Ethel B Dina takes a trip.

'Cooee, my still and sparkling darling,' called Ethel B Dina. 'Look at her – she's smiling.'

The sound that came back shook the walls. It shook Rubbish Island and it shook Bottle Mountain.

'A whale!' said Spokes. 'Now I see why we need the octopuses – to keep the funnel over the whale's blow hole.'

Ethel got the octopuses out of their beds and let them into the sea.

'Brilliant,' said Spokes when he saw them take hold of the funnel. 'The whale will give us a blast of air that will more than fill the balloon.'

Everyone had a job to do. Skittle and
Pinch ran as fast as they could through
the snow to tell Jug and Broom to hold
tight to the balloon.

'When I say the word,' said Spokes to
Ethel B Dina, giving her a tin phone, 'you
tell the whale to blow.'

'Isn't this exciting!' said Ethel B Dina,
as Brew left with Spokes to help him
weigh anchor.

Skittle and Pinch found Jug checking that
the pipe and the funnel were connected.
Broom was holding the balloon.

'What's happening?' said Jug.
'Anything? Something? Nothing?'

'That's a lot of **INGS**,' said Skittle.
'Ethel B Dina says you're to hold very
tight to the balloon.'

Hitch Stitch was standing by with a
big ball of string. It had taken her a long
time to collect and untangle so much.

'Are you sure we'll need the whole ball?' she asked.

'Yes,' said Jug. 'Because once you've tied me to the balloon you must fix the other end firmly somewhere, so the balloon and I don't float away.'

'All right,' said Hitch Stitch. 'I'll put it under this rock.'

'How many fish are blowing into the balloon?' asked Broom.

'None,' said Skittle. 'It's better than fish – it's a whale.'

★

Meanwhile, Captain Spoons was calling
to Spokes.

'Can you hear me, Spokes?'

'Loud and clear, Skipper,' said Spokes.

'All ready this end,' said Captain
Spoons.

Spokes spoke into the tin phone. 'Can
you hear me, Ethel?'

'Yes, my still and sparkling darling,'
replied Ethel B Dina.

'Start singing.'

Ethel sang. The whale let out a blast of warm air that filled the balloon so quickly that everyone was taken by surprise.

Jug raced to fetch his megaphone. His plan was to warn Captain Spoons about rocks and icebergs and tell him which direction to steer in.

Mug and Baby Cup were saying goodbye to Jug.

Captain Spoons yelled, 'Anchors aweigh.'

Spoke and Brew hauled up the anchor.

And then it happened.

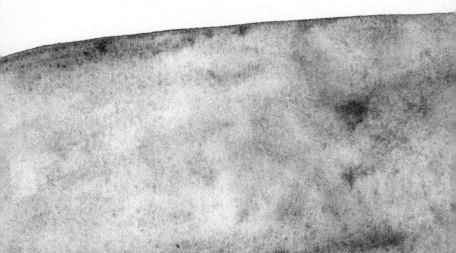

Ethel B Dina, her work done,
arrived in time to see the
air-filled balloon. It looked
wonderful. But then the island
juddered and Ethel B Dina
tripped over the string. It came
free and the balloon began
to fly away. Ethel B Dina
jumped, grabbed the
string, and next second
she found herself
going up, up, up
and up.

Chapter Twelve

Where there's a
bit of a disaster
and the Tindims
don't know
what to do.

And that's
a fact!

'The trouble is,' said Admiral Bonnet, looking up, 'she didn't take the megaphone with her.'

'That's all right,' said Hitch Stitch, 'she can sing.'

Jug shouted, 'Ethel B Dina – can you hear me?'

'Yes,' shouted Ethel B Dina.

'Then sing the directions – full volume!'

It should be explained that Tindims don't know their left from their right. They wouldn't understand, even if you told them.

They would only say, 'Left and right is silly. You only have to turn around and left is right and right is left.'

They had a much more sensible way of doing things. Skittle was standing on one side of the wheelhouse and Pinch on the other. Captain Spoons could see them clearly. When Ethel B Dina sang, he knew exactly which way to steer the island.

'Twenty-five large bottles to Pinch's side,' she trilled.

That's how Tindims measure things: in large and small plastic bottles, when they don't measure in steps.

'Now fifty small to Skittle's side.'

'Full power,' Captain Spoons called down the tube to Spokes.

'Full power it is, Skipper,' said Spokes.

Ethel B Dina sang, 'One hundred large bottles to Pinch's side. A bit more – away from the iceberg with the penguins.'

Admiral Bonnet joined Captain Spoons in the wheelhouse.

'Ethel,' she called
through Jug's megaphone,
'are we in clear waters?'

'Yes, my still and sparkling
darling. We are now. We should pick up
speed.'

The whale was about to make her way
home. But when she heard Ethel B Dina
sing that they should go faster, she knew
she could help.

Suddenly Rubbish Island was whizzing
through the water faster than any island
had ever whizzed before. Every single
Tindim fell head over heels.

'Stars, moon, earth and sea,
All you fishes swimming free.'

Meanwhile, Ethel B Dina was loving being so high. She had the best view. Better still, Rubbish Island was on the move again. She shut her eyes and sang for joy.

Tide turn and waves roll blue,
A song of love, I sing for you.'

It wasn't just little fish that gathered
in shoals to hear her sing. Dolphins
leaped in and out of the waves. Ethel B
Dina sang her heart out as more fish and
sea creatures came to listen.

And so she didn't realise that the
balloon was bobbing about quite slowly
while Rubbish Island, helped by the whale,
was whizzing away from her quite fast.
When she opened her eyes, Rubbish Island
had disappeared.

'Oh, my still and sparkling darlings,'
called Ethel B Dina, 'what about me?'

Chapter Thirteen

Where Ethel B Dina
is left hanging in
the air far away from
Rubbish Island and
the Tindims are sad.

*R*ubbish Island came to rest in a warm blue sea. The Tindims were happy to be there, but terribly sad about Ethel B Dina. Being sad was difficult as it didn't come naturally to them, but losing Ethel B Dina was the most unfunny thing that could have happened.

Captain Spoons and Spokes talked about going backwards. Even if it had been possible, it would take ages.

'It won't bring Ethel B Dina back,' said Captain Spoons. 'The question is how do we go forwards?'

The sunset was a paint pot of pinks and oranges. The Tindims gathered at Turtle Bay and sang a wishing song.

Ethel B Dina, we feel your pain, We want you home with us again...

As they stood looking out to sea, they realised that it was the ebbtide before the Brightsea Festival. The day was almost over. They hadn't opened their sacks. They hadn't made their costumes. And they hadn't put up their decorations. Without the decorations in place they couldn't open Broom's Roo-Roo Pop.

'And without Ethel B Dina,' said Admiral Bonnet, 'how can the Brightsea Festival go ahead at all?'

Just then, Captain Spoons heard singing.

'My still and sparkling darlings, I'm here,' sang Ethel B Dina. 'My arms became too tired to hold on and I fell into the sea.'

'Where is she?' said Skittle.

The Tindims looked but they couldn't see her until Broom cried, 'There she is. A dolphin has rescued her.'

'Ethel, wait there,' called Admiral Bonnet through the megaphone.

'There is nothing else I can do,' sang Ethel B Dina. 'The dolphins can't come further into shore.'

'What about the turtles?' said Brew.

'Ethel, call the turtles,' shouted Admiral Bonnet.

'Oh yes,' said Ethel B Dina. 'Why
didn't I think of that?' And she began to
sing.

Oh turtles of the sea,
 Good friends you are to me.

Help me make it home, be my stepping-stone.

I'll be light on my feet,
 Nimble, quick and neat.

Oh turtles of the sea,
 Dear friends please rescue me.

'It's not my best song,' said Ethel. 'But never mind. If they don't show up, I'm wearing my life saver belt.'

'If she gets close enough, I can hook her in,' said Hitch Stitch.

Captain Spoons was about to shout, 'Sing it again,' when he saw the sea was full of turtles. The tops of their shells were shining on the water.

'Oh, my still and sparkling darlings,' sang Ethel B Dina to the turtles.

Still singing, she hop-skipped from one turtle's shell to another.

Chapter Fourteen

It's time for the
Tindims to put on
a spurt to get the
Brightsea Festival
underway.

he Tindims rushed to greet Ethel B Dina.

'My still and sparkling darlings, it's the ebbtide before the Brightsea Festival. We should be putting up decorations.'

The Tindims ran here and ran there, which meant they ran nowhere at all.

'Wait,' said Mug. 'We must do things properly.' Mug was a sensible Tindim. 'First, we must put up the decorations before it's too dark to see.'

Tindims are hard workers. That is why they get on so well. And they find each other funny and know how to laugh.

Now Ethel
B Dina was
safe, there
was a lot to
laugh about.

That night, if you could have glimpsed
Rubbish Island, you'd have seen it sparkle
and shine as bright as a star that had
fallen to earth. This only happened on
the two days of the Brightsea Festival.
Spokes had made a special banner
that he'd hung up. It said *HAPPY*
BRIGHTSEA DAY TO YOU A.

There wasn't room for
the last word, but every
Tindim knew it was
supposed to say
'Happy Brightsea
Day to you ALL.'

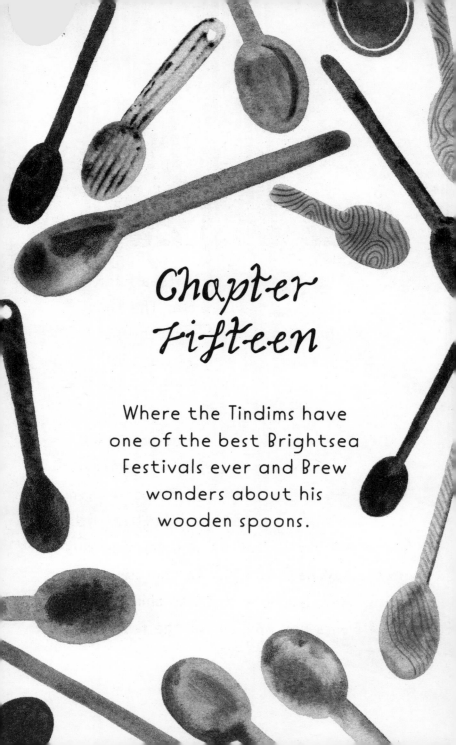

Chapter Fifteen

Where the Tindims have
one of the best Brightsea
Festivals ever and Brew
wonders about his
wooden spoons.

_T_he day of the Brightsea Festival dawned, daisy-fresh. The snow had melted and Rubbish Island was in full bloom. The trees were in blossom and the plants were green and happy.

Bottle Mountain was a mass of little pink starflowers. Just before the snow had come, Granny Gull and Barnacle Bow had filled a great many bottles with earth and planted seeds in them. The tiny plants had been waiting for the cold snap to be over. Now the sun was shining and the flowers had opened for the festival.

Mug decided that the
sacks would be handed
out today as there had
been no time the day before.
The Tindims went to find
a quiet place to work
on their fish costumes.

As Pinch only had paws, and glue and fur isn't much fun, Skittle and Brew were allowed to help him. Brew wanted to go as a rainbow starfish. There were lots of coloured plastic bags in his sack. Skittle had heaps of tin foil. Pinch had four small hoops.

It was a lovely day for making fish costumes and being thoughtful about the sea. Each Tindim took time to hope that the Long Legs would stop throwing things away.

This was it. The big moment when
everyone arrived in their fish costumes
for the feast. Broom came as an eel and
brought as many bottles of Roo-Roo Pop
as he could carry. Ethel B Dina wore
a mackerel costume with a turtle hat.
Mug and Jug came as a whale (which is
not actually a fish), Mug was the front
and Jug was the back. Baby Cup was a
minnow.

Brew had made a very good rainbow starfish costume. Everyone agreed there was something special about Skittle's glittering angelfish. And Pinch was the best pufferfish anyone had ever seen.

Brew's rainbow starfish costume was the winner. Only he had used every piece of treasure in his sack. His prize was a bag of buttons.

'Speech,' called the Tindims.

Brew stood on his chair. 'I think there might be magic in my wooden spoon,' he said. 'I waved it over my sack and it worked – my costume won.'

The Tindims ate and laughed and danced until nearly moontide when Admiral Bonnet handed out small paper boats. Each Tindim wrote on their boat what they hoped for in the new year. It wouldn't be right to tell you what they wished for. Enough to say that solving the problem of Bottle Mountain was high on Captain Spoons' list.

Admiral Bonnet thanked the sea for looking after them. She thanked the whale for bringing the island into warmer seas. And she thanked the dolphins and the turtles for saving Ethel B Dina.

The Tindims took their paper boats to the water's edge and silently

watched them float away. Once they'd
disappeared, everyone went happily home
to bed.

Skittle called out of her window,
'Goodnight, Brew.'

'Goodnight, Skittle,' Brew called back.
'Do you think my wooden spoon is magic?'

'No,' said Skittle sleepily. 'I think you
are the magic.

'Goodnight, Pinch.'

'Goodnight,' said Pinch. 'I wonder what
will happen tomorrow?'

'One thing I know,' said Skittle, 'is
that it will be different from today.
Maybe tomorrow will be the year we meet
the Long Legs.'

'*That's a fact*,' said Pinch.

'Rubbish today is treasure tomorrow'

You can make pencil holders, or a plant holder from the bottom of cut-off plastic bottles.

Poke holes in the bottom if you're making a plant holder so water can drain.

Make your own Tindim from a loo roll, a washing-up bottle and any bits of fabric and paper. Where do they live on Rubbish Island?

Help keep beaches clean!
Tell the Long Legs
to pick up litter
and take it home!